YOU MIGHT BE SPECIAL!

For Chloe and Ollie, two kids who I suspect are special.
Otherwise, how would they have grown up so fast? — K.K.

For Sophie and Beatrix, the most fantastic
creatures of all — M.C.

Published in Canada and the U.S. by Kids Can Press Ltd.
25 Dockside Drive, Toronto, ON M5A 0B5

Kids Can Press is a Corus Entertainment Inc. company
www.kidscanpress.com

The artwork in this book was rendered digitally.
The text is set in HandySans.

Edited by Yasemin Uçar
Designed by Barb Kelly

Printed and bound in Buji, Shenzhen, China, in 3/2021 by
WKT Company

CM 21 0 9 8 7 6 5 4 3 2 1

**Library and Archives Canada Cataloguing in
Publication**

Title: You might be special! / written by Kerri Kokias ;
illustrated by Marcus Cutler.
Names: Kokias, Kerri, author. | Cutler, Marcus, 1978 –
illustrator.
Identifiers: Canadiana 20200365452 | ISBN
9781525303333 (hardcover)
Classification: LCC PZ7.1.K65 You 2021 | DDC j813/.6
— dc23

Kids Can Press gratefully acknowledges that the land
on which our office is located is the traditional territory of
many nations, including the Mississaugas of the Credit,
the Anishnabeg, the Chippewa, the Haudenosaunee and
the Wendat peoples, and is now home to many
diverse First Nations, Inuit and Métis peoples.

We thank the Government of Ontario, through Ontario
Creates; the Ontario Arts Council; the Canada Council
for the Arts; and the Government of Canada for
supporting our publishing activity.

YOU MIGHT BE SPECIAL!

TAKE THE QUIZ TO FIND OUT...?

WRITTEN BY
KERRI KOKIAS

ILLUSTRATED BY
MARCUS CUTLER

KIDS CAN PRESS

Do you ever feel like you're different from everyone else?

Does it sometimes seem like there's no one quite like you?

You might be **SPECIAL!**

Take this quiz to find out ...

Are you usually gentle and kind?

Do you sometimes need a little quiet time?

Are you crazy about rainbows?

Do you gallop or trot on four legs and have a horn in the center of your forehead?

Are you sure?
Then you must not be a ...

UNICORN!

Okay. Well, don't worry.
Unicorns are pretty special, but
I can see that **YOU** are gentle
and kind **AND** you don't have
to worry about accidentally
poking things with your horn.

I'll try again ...

Are you strong?

Are you brave?

Do you sometimes feel grumpy even when you don't want to be?

Can you cook hot dogs with your breath?

No? Because I was thinking you might be a ...

DRAGON!

Silly me. Of course you're not a dragon! **YOU** are strong and brave **AND** others feel safe around you — even when you're in a bad mood.

Gulp!

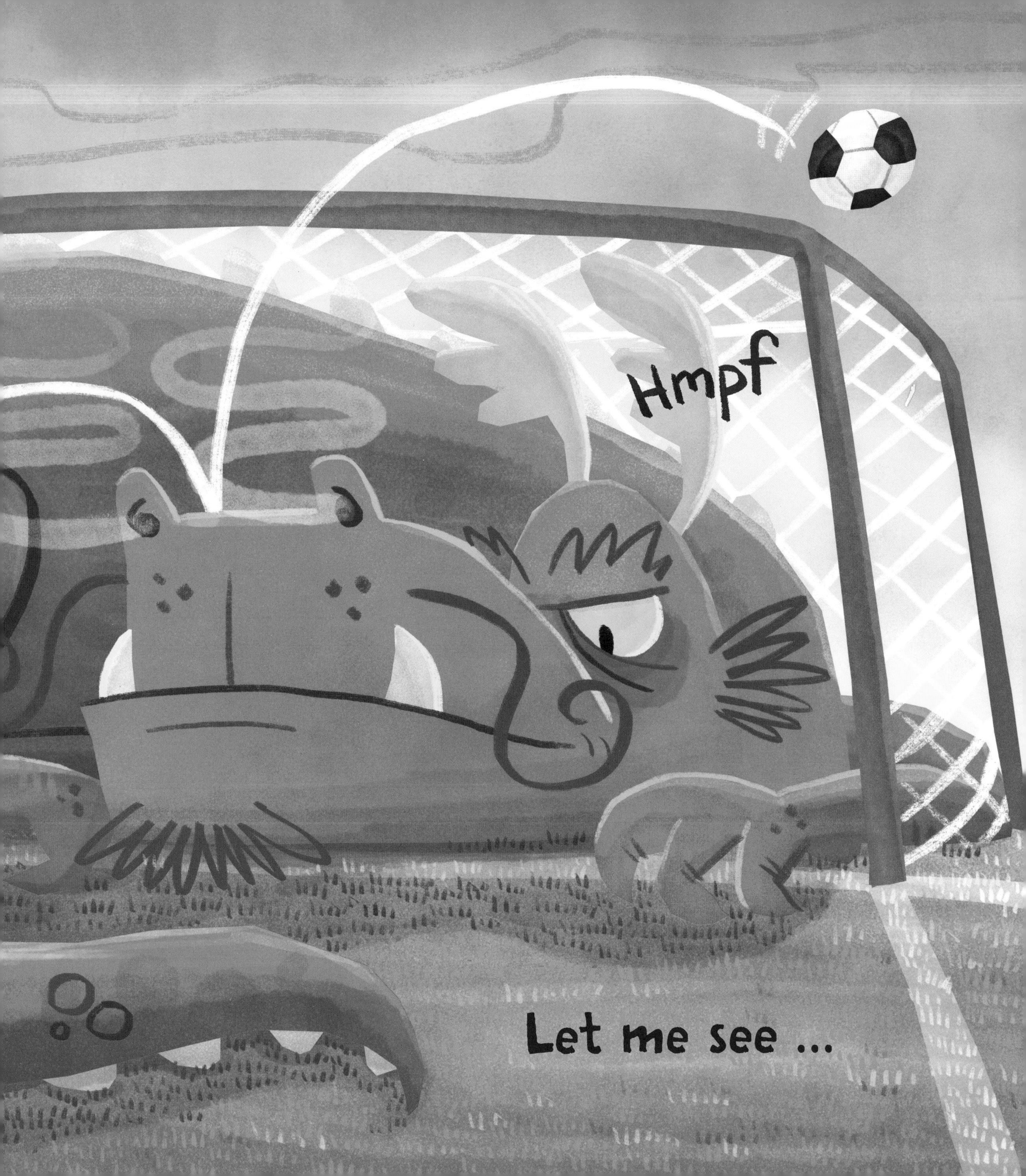

Let me see ...

Do you enjoy spending time with friends?

Are you usually quite cheerful?

Is it sometimes hard for you to sit still?

Have you ever noticed that most butterflies are bigger than you?

Oh. Then I don't think you're a ...

Hmm ...

Are your feet bigger
than they used to be?

Are you growing
taller and taller?

Do you
sometimes smell
just a little funny?

Do you spend most of your time
playing hide-and-seek
barefoot in muddy forests?

Okay, it doesn't sound
like you're a ...

SASQUATCH!

I'm sorry — I should have noticed that YOU are really quite clean. (But good job on all the growing!)

I'll keep trying ...

Do you like to
stay up late?

Can you
run fast and
jump high?

Are you sometimes wild and crazy?

Do people run away when they see
your furry face and pointy teeth?

Phew! Then you're not a ...

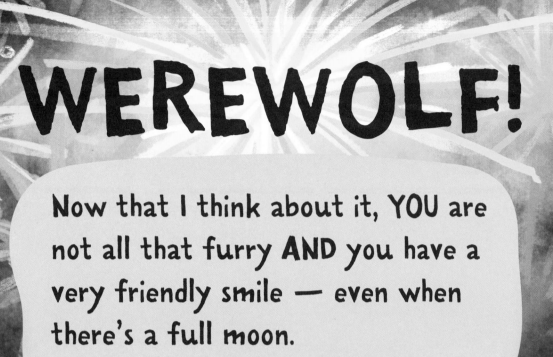

Are you sometimes a little bit shy?

Is one of your top ten favorite colors blue?

Do you like to take long baths?

Can you hold your breath under water for at least twelve and a half hours?

Right. Then you're probably not a ...

MERMAID!

But that's a good thing because YOU can play in the water AND on land. Plus, you don't smell fishy at all!

What **ARE** you?

What in the **WORLD** could you be???